Norman
the Norman
From Normandy

Philip Ardagh

Norman the Norman from Normandy

Illustrated by
Tom Morgan-Jones

Barrington Stoke

First published in 2017 in Great Britain by
Barrington Stoke Ltd
18 Walker Street, Edinburgh, EH3 7LP

www.barringtonstoke.co.uk

Text © 2017 Philip Ardagh
Illustrations © 2017 Tom Morgan-Jones

A CIP catalogue record for this book is available
from the British Library upon request

ISBN: 978-1-78112-697-4

Printed in China by Leo

This book is in a super readable format for young readers
beginning their independent reading journey.

*For my mother and father,
who read me books
and told me stories.
Thank you.*

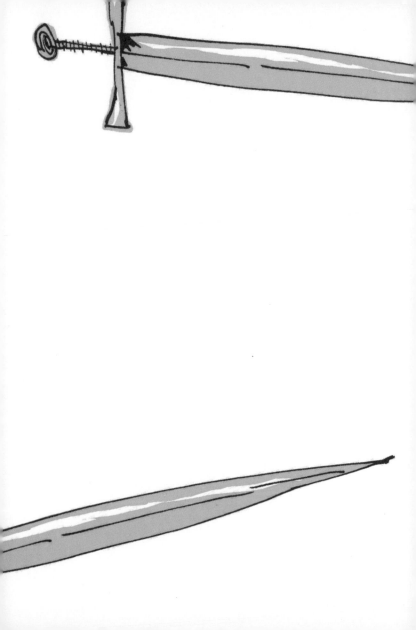

Contents

Chapter 1

Out Come the Swords

Norman the Norman was from Normandy.

Here's Normandy, or a small part of it. With cows.

Here's Norman.

Here's a squirrel eating an acorn
(because squirrels are cute).

Norman the Norman from Normandy got up every morning, wearing nothing but his helmet and his chainmail, and ran around his bedroom waving his sword. He was careful not to break anything ... but often not quite careful enough.

CRASH!

See what I mean?

Norman's sword was a great big Norman broad sword. It used to be Great Big Norman's great big Norman broad sword. Great Big Norman was Norman's father. Like his sword, he was broad. He would STILL be Norman's father if he hadn't got into a fight with ten Bretons from Brittany.

When Great Big Norman first met the Bretons, they all got along fine, laughing and joking and talking about battles they'd been in. Fine, that is, until Great Big Norman trod on one of the Breton's toes. It hurt, but Great Big Norman didn't notice what he'd done, so he didn't say sorry. Then the Bretons made the mistake of TELLING him – not asking him – to apologise.

A fight broke out. Fists flew.
Furniture flew. A passing pigeon flew.
That squirrel from earlier got flu. And
then out came the swords.

The fight didn't last long. Great Big Norman managed to kill seven of the ten Bretons from Brittany, which left three Bretons to chop Great Big Norman into three smaller pieces.

One piece each, which was only fair.

But the Bretons were VERY impressed with how brave Great Big Norman had been and how well he had fought. As a mark of respect, they each wanted to bury him on their own land. But none of them could agree on who should get his great big body and all the glory.

So what did they do?

You guessed it. They buried the three bits of Great Big Norman in three different graves, on their three different bits of land. And when that was done, they sent Norman his father's sword and they all signed their names at the bottom of a WE ARE SORRY FOR YOUR LOSS tapestry.

WE ARE SORRY
FOR YOUR LOSS
ERIC THE FEARFUL
DUC DE QUACK
BERNARD THE BRETON

Chapter 2

No More Little Norman

When the package arrived in the post, Norman didn't find it too hard to guess what was in it. The great big broad sword shape of the package was a clue. And, after that, everything changed. For starters, no one called him

'Little Norman' any more. That's what they had called him when Great Big Norman was still around. Now Great Big Norman was no more.

This was also the day that Norman swore to visit each of his father's three graves to pay his respects.

"Stop swearing, Norman," his mother said.

Norman's mother was still VERY much alive. Her name was Norma the Norman from Normandy. She was a very strong and powerful woman. She bent bent iron bars straight for a living. Her sister Nora bent straight iron bars bent, so they were never out of work. Norman was sad that his dad was dead but he was also proud that his dad had died fighting. After all, that's how most soldiers want to die.

That, or of old age surrounded by loved ones. Or in the middle of a nice big meal of their favourite food.

Splat. Face first in the gravy.

Norma used to give Norman an egg for breakfast every morning. And every breakfast, Norman used his father's sword to chop the top off the egg. And every morning he ended up chopping rather a lot of other things too. That's why most things in the kitchen were either stuck together with glue or tied together with string. And why their servant, Bog, used to crawl around the kitchen on all-fours until after 9.00 a.m., just to be on the safe side.

But now Norman was about to leave home.

"Good luck, dear," his mum said. "Be sure to say hello to all three bits of your father from me." She handed Norman a large cloth tied into a bundle.

"What's this?" he asked.

"It's a large cloth tied into a bundle," she said.

"I can see that," Norman said. "But what's it for?"

"It's full of useful things," she said.

Norma the Norman from Normandy picked up her son (Little) Norman the Norman from Normandy as if he were as light as a rice-cake. Then she hugged him almost as hard as a python squeezing its prey. "Squeeeeeeeeeeeeeeeeeeee!" she said.

Norman went almost as red as a Coke can, but he didn't mind because he knew that this was a loving hug. He kissed his mother on the cheek. It was a bit like kissing a bag of very lovable walnuts.

And then Norman jumped up onto Truffle and was ready to go.

Truffle was a tame wild boar, which meant that he wasn't really wild any more. He was more of a not-so-wild boar. But he did have impressive tusks, was VERY bristly and could make some seriously impressive grunts and squeals.

Because Norman the Norman from Normandy was far too small to ride a horse, or a pony or a donkey, he went about by not-so-wild boar. Truffle was an uncomfortable and grunty ride, but Norman loved him.

Chapter 3

Rocks and Buns

Norman looked quite a sight as he left that day on Truffle's back, with the cloth tied into a bundle on HIS back and his father's HUGE sword in his hand.

Off he trotted.

Norman was a familiar sight in the nearby villages. Villagers would greet him with a friendly jeer or throw a rock or two at him. There weren't THAT many good-sized rocks to throw so, sometimes, a villager would throw a rock and wait for it to bounce off Norman.

Then they'd run up, snatch the rock and scuttle back far enough to get in another good throw.

To tell the truth, Norman quite enjoyed the attention and the 'clang' if one of the villagers scored a bullseye when their rock hit his helmet. The villagers were always VERY careful not to hit Truffle by mistake. Even a not-so-wild boar could get VERY angry if hit by a rock.

Norman the Norman from Normandy hadn't travelled for more than a few hours on his quest when he was hit by a different kind of missile – a very stale bun. The bun was so stale that it was almost as HARD as a rock.

It was thrown by a boy of about Norman's age, but this boy was much taller than him – which wasn't hard. His name was Albert, which he said like 'Alber', as if he couldn't be bothered to add the 't' to the end. He was the son of a big local landowner, and his clothes were very fine.

"Hi, Norman!" Albert shouted. "Where are you going?"

"I'm off to visit my father's graves," Norman shouted back. "All three of them."

"To avenge your father's death?" Albert called.

Norman had no idea what 'avenge' meant – it means 'to get revenge' – but he didn't want to admit that he had no idea, so he shouted, "Maybe!"

"Good luck with that," Albert said. And he laughed.

Chapter 4

Norman the Norman in Brittany

That night, Norman and Truffle slept under the stars. For such a bristly pig, Truffle was very huggable. Neither pig nor boy was stupid, so they snuggled together to keep each other warm.

It became very cold in the night, and the bundle Norman's mum had given him wasn't big enough to contain a blanket. Or a tent.

The next morning, Norman got up
in his chainmail, yawned, stretched, put
on his helmet, picked up his father's old
sword and swung it about.

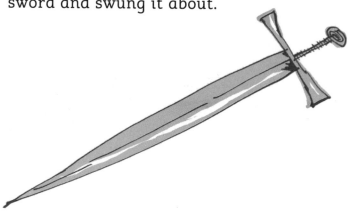

It sliced off the branch of a tree just above him, and this landed on his head. If Norman hadn't been wearing his helmet, he'd have knocked himself out cold. As it was, he was now seeing more stars than he'd seen all night.

Truffle was awake too, and he was off snuffling for acorns with that impressive snout of his. Soon both boar and boy were ready to go.

After a few more days and nights, and a few minor adventures – one of which involved a cabbage thief and another a trained jackdaw – Norman the Norman from Normandy arrived in Brittany.

Chapter 5

The First Grave Mistake

The first person Norman went to visit was Eric the Fearful. He parked Truffle out of sight around the corner from Eric the Fearful's castle, and gave him a large bag of acorns to chew while he visited the first of his father's three graves.

Norman was very aware that he was SO much smaller than his father. He didn't want to look even less impressive by turning up on piggy back.

And so, Norman marched up to the castle gates and banged on them with the handle of his sword. A little door opened and the Captain of the Guard stepped out. "Yes?" he demanded.

"I am here to visit the grave of my father," said Norman.

The Captain of the Guard glared at him as if he were a small piece of very common fly poo. "And who might your father be?"

"Great Big Norman the Norman from Normandy," Norman said. He waved the huge broad sword above his head, and almost knocked himself off his feet with the weight of it.

The colour drained from the Captain's face. The truth be told, it drained from all of his body, right the way down to his feet but – because he was covered in chainmail – only his face showed.

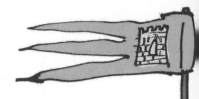

His whole expression changed too. He was still looking down at Norman, what with Norman being SO much smaller than him, but he was no longer looking down ON him. His eyes were now filled with respect.

"Please wait here!" the Captain of the Guard said, and he rushed off to find Eric the Fearful.

Eric rushed down to greet Big Norman the Norman's son. "You're a little smaller than your father," he observed.

"Most people are," Norman said. "He was built like a castle."

"And he was also very brave," said Eric.

"Indeed," Norman said. "But where is your bit of him buried?"

"Over there," said Eric, and he pointed to a rather nice spot under an oak tree behind Norman.

Norman rested his broad sword on his shoulder and turned to take a look. And, as he turned, he accidentally chopped off Eric the Fearful's head. This

was unfortunate enough, but even more unfortunate was that he didn't notice what he'd done because his back was turned.

So Norman didn't say "Sorry!" He was already striding over to the grave where his father's legs were buried.

When the Captain of the Guard came out to find Eric the Fearful, he found

that his master's head was no longer
attached to his master's body. He looked
over to Norman who had finished paying
his respects to his father's legs and feet
and was now on the move again.

"Like father like son!" the Captain of the Guard muttered under his breath. "Cool as a cucumber!"

The Captain ordered two of his men to carry Eric's body inside, and then he went and got a large dustpan and brush for the head. He used the dustpan with the long, upright handle, to save him from having to bend down. He couldn't wait to tell the other captains of the other guards that his master had had the honour of being killed by Great Big Norman the Norman's son Norman!

Chapter 6

The Second Grave Mistake

Norman was blissfully unaware of what he'd done as he headed off in the direction of the Château of the Duc de Quack.

Duc is French for 'Duke', so there was nothing silly about his name at all. So no giggling. "Quack!"

On the way, Norman rescued eleven nuns from a burning nunnery. He rescued two of them twice, because they'd gone back in to rescue the nunnery cat, Salmon. Norman ended up having to rescue Salmon too.

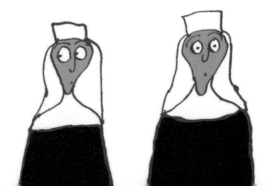

Norman also helped a village that was living in fear of a great big snake that simply sat there and stared at them but never did anything. The snake turned out to be an old fire hose that someone had drawn a pair of googly eyes on.

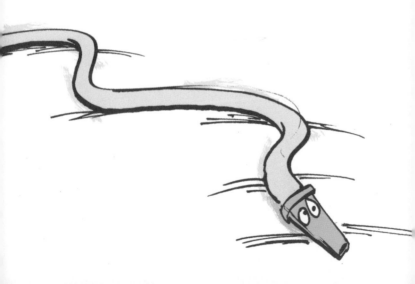

And he saved the life of an enormous toad that was so grateful it decided to hop up on the top of Norman's helmet and enjoy the ride.

When Norman arrived at the Duc's château, Truffle was quite happy to stay out of sight, but the toad insisted on coming in with him. They found the Duc de Quack in the middle of his garden, in

the middle of a red rose bush. He was having a fight with the bush because it had been REALLY annoying him. The bush seemed to be winning – the Duc de Quack was surrounded by thorny stems. His Head Gardener was watching and 'tutting' from a safe distance.

"Hello," said Norman. "I'm here to see some of my father."

"Some of him?" the Duc snarled, and he punched a rose so hard that the red petals scattered like a nosebleed.

"He was Great Big Norman of Normandy."

The Duc de Quack stood stock still. Norman's words drifted on a light breeze into the Head Gardener's hairy ears.

"His g-g-grave is over there," said the Duc. "I'll join you just as soon as I've destroyed this bush."

"Let me help!" said Norman, who was a polite young Norman. He slashed at the thorny stems with his sword, then turned before his handiwork was done. So he didn't see that he'd also cut the Duc de Quack in two. But the toad saw and he went "Ribbit!" because he'd spent too much time with frogs.

"Wow!" the Head Gardener said. Then he ordered the Gardener and Under Gardener to get two wheelbarrows – one for the Duc's top half, and one for his bottom half, which included his actual bottom.

After Norman had visited the grave of his father's torso and arms, and muttered a few sad words, such as, "Miss you, Dad," and "Mum says hi," he now headed for the third and final grave.

On the way, Norman pulled a thorn from a lion's paw, stuck a thorn in a different lion's paw – there was a circus in town – and then he rescued a thirsty princess who'd fallen down a well.

Chapter 7

The Third Grave Mistake

The third and final grave was inside
a stone casket in the middle of a
courtyard in the middle of a castle. This
castle's owner, Bernard the Breton, was
NOT about to let Norman inside.

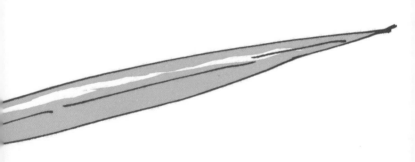

That's because news travels fast.

The carrier pigeon who delivered the message that Norman was on his way had stopped for two fingers of KitKat and a cup of sweet tea. But, even so, Bernard knew ALL about how Norman the

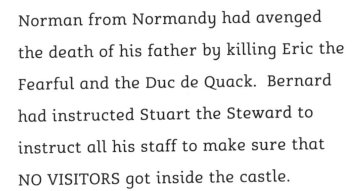

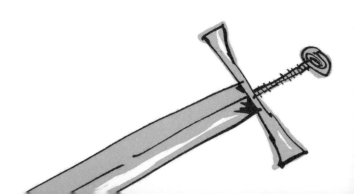

Norman from Normandy had avenged the death of his father by killing Eric the Fearful and the Duc de Quack. Bernard had instructed Stuart the Steward to instruct all his staff to make sure that NO VISITORS got inside the castle.

"Go away!" Bernard shouted from the highest window in the highest tower when he saw Norman climbing off Truffle's back with the toad on his helmet.

"Hello, Monsieur Bernard!" Norman shouted with a friendly wave or two.

Well, he thought they were friendly waves but one wave was with the hand Norman was holding his father's broad sword in, so Bernard the Breton thought it was a threatening sword-shake.

"Pleeeeeeease go away!" Bernard shouted. Bernard the Breton was always scared, ever since his wife had vanished after making a rude comment about the local witch's curtains.

The toad, which Norman had named Toad, hopped off Norman's head and managed to find his way into the castle by squeezing through gaps like only toads and frogs and snails and mice – and any other squeeze-through-tiny-spaces animals I've forgotten – can. He hopped up the winding spiral stairs of the highest tower and into the room where Bernard was standing.

Toad hopped up onto the window sill to get eye-to-eye with Bernard the Breton. Bernard looked at Toad. Toad looked at Bernard and went "Ribbit".

Now – like most people – Bernard the Breton found it hard to tell the difference between frogs and toads, but what he DID know was that frogs, not toads, went "Ribbit".

Bernard ALSO knew that witches and wicked stepmothers and so on often turned princes and princesses into FROGS.

Now, Bernard had never considered his wife to be a princess. She reminded him more of a very cuddly owl. But he loved cuddly owls and he loved his wife. And he missed her. And she had disappeared after she'd upset that witch. Could the witch have turned HER into a frog?

Could this be her? Had she found her way back to him?

There was only one way to find out. He would kiss her. That should work. That's what turned enchanted frogs back into their proper, human form.

Far down below, outside the castle,
Norman was still waving frantically ...
when he saw ... No, it couldn't be?
Surely not? That was Toad with Bernard
the Breton? It was. It was his new
friend Toad!

"Coooooooeeeee!" Norman waved.

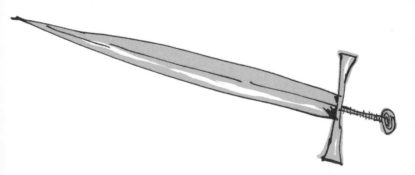

At that moment, Bernard's lips touched the top of Toad's head. Unfortunately, Toad was a very poisonous toad. He was so poisonous that even people who made poison-tipped darts for their blowpipes were very polite to him and would only go near him if they were wearing three pairs of gloves and were wrapped in a mattress. In another room.

Bernard the Breton made a noise like a washing machine stuffed with dirty pants, and toppled out of the highest window in the highest tower. He left Toad just enough time to hop back onto the sill.

Fortunately, Bernard landed in the back of an empty cart. The fall still killed him, but it made it very easy for

Stuart the Steward to wheel his body
to the family chapel, and there wasn't
nearly so much mess for the servants to
clear up.

Stuart ordered the gatekeepers
to open the gates and let the son of
Great Big Norman the Norman from
Normandy in to see his father's grave
at once, before he gave anyone else that
look …

The steward had assumed that the look he'd seen on Norman's face was a special killer look. In fact, it was one of surprise on spotting Toad. But Stuart the Steward didn't want to be looked at in that way. No, sir. So Norman was welcomed in, and he paid his respects to his father's head. And he told him that Norma the Norman sent her love, too.

Norman was delighted by the kind reception he'd had from all three Bretons who'd buried all three bits of his dad. And so he decided to head for home on Truffle with his new friend Toad.

Chapter 8

The Avenger of Death

As he made his way back across Brittany,
Norman saved a fish from drowning,
helped a chicken cross the road, and
showed a peasant farmer how to tie his
shoe laces. He'd already done all the big
heroic deeds on his way there, so now he
was running out of good deeds to do.

When Norman crossed back into Normandy, Truffle had a new spring in his not-so-wild-boar step. Truffle was probably biased, but Normandy acorns tasted SO much better than the Brittany ones! Toad was happy wherever he was, as long as he could spend most of his time sitting on Norman's Norman helmet.

Albert – you remember him, the rich kid who didn't bother to say the 't' at the end of his name – was one of the first people to greet Norman. Instead of throwing a stale bun at him, he gave him a special kind of pastry that Normans get excited about.

"Welcome back!" he cried. "So you DID avenge the death of your father!"

"Did I?" Norman said. He still didn't know what 'avenge' meant.

When Norman reached the villages near his home, none of the villagers threw old rocks at him, scurried over, picked them up and threw them again. No, this boy was a hero. He had avenged his father's death AND upheld the honour of Normandy against Brittany. They now had brand NEW rocks to throw, hundreds of them, all the perfect size and in polished wooden buckets. Only the best rocks would do for Norman ...

... but their job was made all the harder now Norman had a toad on his head. Now they had to avoid upsetting the not-so-wild boar AND the poisonous-looking toad.

Chapter 9

Welcome Home, Norman!

When, at last, Norman reached home, the squirrel had got better from its bout of flu.

If you don't remember the squirrel
or the flu, or just the squirrel and
not the flu, or just the flu and not the
squirrel, then turn back to Chapter 1.

Norma, Norman's mother, was
waiting for him. She was picking up
bent bars from a pile of bent bars,
straightening them and putting them in
another pile. Her sister Nora was then
taking them, bending them and putting
them back in the first pile.

"You're home!" Norma cried, and she kissed her boy on the top of his head. Or where the top of his head would be if he weren't wearing a helmet. With a toad on top. So in fact Norma kissed Toad instead ...

... which wasn't a problem. This is Norma we're talking about. Norma the Norman from Normandy. Hers is one tough family. Don't believe me? You should meet her son, Norman. He's a hero and a fighter like his dad.

The only thing is, he doesn't know it.

An Afterword

Are you wondering what was in the large cloth tied into a bundle that Norman's mother, Norma, gave Norman before he set off on his travels? It was a slightly smaller cloth, in case he lost the first one. And you can guess what was inside that.

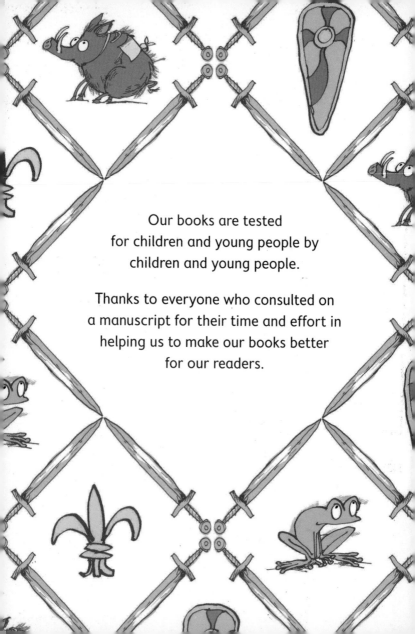

Our books are tested
for children and young people by
children and young people.

Thanks to everyone who consulted on
a manuscript for their time and effort in
helping us to make our books better
for our readers.